The
Adirondack
Kids® #4

The Great Train Robbery

Justin

Gary Van...

by Justin & Gary VanRiper
Illustrations by Carol VanRiper

Adirondack Kids Press
Camden, New York

The Adirondack Kids® #4
The Great Train Robbery

Justin & Gary VanRiper
Copyright © 2004. All rights reserved.

First Paperback Printing, March 2004
Second Paperback Printing, July 2005

Cover illustration by Susan Loeffler
Illustrated by Carol VanRiper
Cover Design and Production by Nancy Did It!, Blossvale, NY

Photographs of Theodore Roosevelt as a boy, in a guide boat
and in the White House appear with permission:
Theodore Roosevelt Collection, Harvard College Library,
Harvard University, Cambridge, Massachusetts 02138.
Photograph of Mike Cronin and his horse drawn carriage
appears with permission: Adirondack Museum,
Blue Mountain Lake, New York 12812.
Photograph of North Creek Railroad Depot, March 4, 1934
by John Cornwall, used by permission: Helen Cornwall
Portrait of Justin & Gary VanRiper ©2003 by Carol VanRiper

Published by
Adirondack Kids Press
39 Second Street
Camden, New York 13316

Printed in the United States of America
by Patterson Printing, Michigan

ISBN 0-9707044-3-7

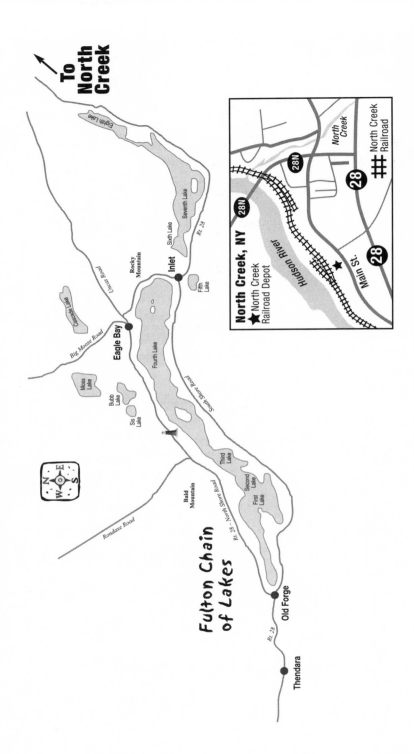

Contents

For our many new friends
in the warm Adirondack community
of North Creek

CHAPTER I

All Aboard!

"What's the big surprise?" Justin Robert asked his cousin, Zack. "You have to tell me before the train leaves." He looked toward the North Creek Depot Museum. People were moving quickly out from under the porch's gable roof into the hot summer sun. "Come on, Nick. Come on, Jackie." Neither of them were among the many passengers making their way along the station's long wood plank platform with tickets in hand. Justin took a deep breath and sighed. "They're going to miss the surprise *and* the robbery."

Zack wasn't really listening. He was staring at Justin's strange-looking watch. "How can you even tell what time it is without any numbers on that thing?" he asked.

Justin looked down at his timepiece. The large pocket watch his grandfather had just given him nearly filled the palm of his hand. It was a family treasure. Shaped like a miniature flying saucer, the gold casing was smooth on the bottom, and on top featured a raised engraving of a white-tailed deer, jumping over a log in the forest. "It's easy to tell what

"All aboard," said the conductor.

time it is," he said, and pushed a small latch. The watch yawned open like a clamshell.

"Awesome," said Zack. "So, what time is it?"

"It's almost one o'clock," said Justin, and hesitated, "I think."

The black numbers on the white watch face were Roman Numerals. They were exactly like the numbers on the giant clock at the top of the town hall back in Justin's hometown. The big hand was almost on the twelve, which looked like a large X followed by two capital I's. The little hand pointed toward a line that looked like a single capital I.

It wasn't easy to figure out the numbers at first and took some getting used to, but he loved it. The antique timepiece was the first really important thing his grandfather had ever given to him.

"Take good care of this watch," his grandfather had told him just before he left camp at Eagle Bay to visit his cousin, Zachary Casey, in North Creek. "Someday you may give it to your grandson."

It wasn't cool like Jackie's sports watch that glowed in the dark and had more than a dozen colored buttons on it. It was cool in a different way. It was handsome and heavy and it felt like he really had something impressive in his hand.

"All aboard!" The conductor bellowed the command.

Dozens of summer tourists began forming orderly lines along the platform, ready for their turn to climb up one of the short ramps provided at each end of the train.

Justin noticed the conductor pull out a pocket watch on a chain similar to his own. *His is silver, mine is gold,* he thought. It gave him a good excuse to proudly pop open his watch again. The big hand was now directly on the XII and the small hand on the I. "It's exactly one o'clock," he said. "Right on time." He snapped the lid closed and put the watch with its long gold chain back into his pocket.

Locomotive No. 5019 glowed under the bright July sky. The mammoth blue-and-gray machine accented with yellow stripes and rails bore the words **UPPER HUDSON RIVER** on its side. Five long passenger coaches, each painted forest green and Johnsburg brown, sat in line coupled to the engine. At the rear was an open-air caboose that looked more like a deck encompassed by a simple wood railing.

Justin noticed an engineer in white-and-blue pin-striped overalls start up the steps of the steep ladder to take his place high above in the locomotive's cab. He looked again for some sign of his friends. "Where are they?" he said aloud in frustration.

A familiar voice called out from somewhere behind him. "Hey Justin, are you guys coming or not?" It was Nick Barnes, one of his two best friends in the whole world, already in line holding a fresh bag of popcorn and about to board the train. Jackie Salsberry, his other best friend, was right next to him, smiling.

"What took you so long?" asked Justin, as he and Zack ran over to join them.

"It wathn't me, it wath her," Nick mumbled, his

4

mouth full of popcorn. He swallowed and pointed at Jackie. "She was reading all the stuff in the museum about how a United States President shot 26 buffalo right here in North Creek, New York."

Jackie's smile disappeared and she nodded in dismay. "Weren't you paying attention at all? I said 'President McKinley was shot in Buffalo, New York. He died, and Theodore Roosevelt became the 26th President right here in North Creek.' You'll see during the reenactment on Sunday."

Nick shrugged his shoulders and hopped up into the train. He stopped abruptly at the top step and looked back at his friends. "So – where is the big surprise?"

CHAPTER II

Hat Trick

Justin, Jackie and Zack followed Nick onto the train.

"Let Zack get in front of us," said Justin. "He rides the train all the time and knows the best seats."

Zack was the oldest in the group, but was also the shortest and thinnest among them. He easily slipped into the lead and guided his guests quickly down the center aisle of passenger cars one and two, past row after row of blue-and-purple seats which were filling up fast with adults and kids carrying backpacks, cameras and coolers. "Here," he said, and jumped into one of the large padded blue seats in coach number three. "We made it." He placed his engineer's cap and red bandanna on the seat next to him and opened the fringed shade for a clear view out the large rectangular window.

Nick plopped down next to him. Zack managed to pick up his cap and bandanna just before he landed.

Justin and Jackie jumped into the large double seat that faced them. The backs of their roll-over seats were so wide and high, it was like they had their own private room.

Jackie looked over at Zack. "How long did you say your dad has been a conductor on the train?" she asked.

"He only does it on long weekends," Zack said. "He really loves helping out with the train robberies, so I get to ride the train a lot. His regular job is building boats."

"It was really nice of your parents to invite all of us this weekend," Jackie said. "It's not that far away from Eagle Bay, but I've never been to North Creek before. And I can't wait to meet President Roosevelt."

"That will be okay, but I can't wait for the shootout," said Justin. "We've all been on the Adirondack train in Thendara when it was robbed. And I've been in North Creek a few times. But this will be the first time I'll be robbed here."

Nick looked bored and the train hadn't even left the station. "How far is that Rapper place from North Creek?" he asked. "Don't you all get bored riding these trains? The robberies don't seem very real to me."

"It's entertainment," said Jackie. "It's not supposed to scare kids to death. Can't you enjoy it and just have fun – use your imagination?"

"You mean, just *pretend* it's real?" said Nick.

"You don't have to ruin it for everyone else," Jackie said.

Nick stuck his head out into the aisle. There were kids everywhere. Several wore cowboy hats and some had little guns and holsters. They were already looking expectantly out their windows for bad guys.

7

"Bang!" yelled Nick, and all three of his friends jumped. So did a little boy sitting directly across the aisle who leaped into his mother's lap.

Jackie looked over at Nick and shook her head. "That was just plain mean," she said. "I'll get you back." She paused, and raised an eyebrow. "You know I will."

Justin kept looking at the cap in his cousin's lap. "Are you going to wear that hat, or just hold it?"

The red handkerchief that was still tucked inside the cap began to move. Justin looked puzzled. "Hey, how did you do that?"

"I told you I had a surprise," said Zack. "It's not really a big surprise – it's more like a small, fuzzy one."

"It's a kitten," said Jackie. "How cuuute."

"Your lips look just like a fish when you say the word *cute* that way," said Nick.

Jackie squinted her eyes and glared at him.

Nick shrugged. "I'm just using my imagination," he said.

"Why did I have to leave Dax back at your house?" Justin asked his cousin. He missed his faithful calico companion. "You said I couldn't bring a cat on the train."

"This is totally different," said Zack. "Hudson is our new railroad cat, and today is her adoption day." He gave the kitten a small treat, one of several stored at the bottom of the cap. "The engineer is going to take her home after the ride today. We have to get her used to riding on the train."

"How old is she?" Jackie asked.

The tiny gray kitten poked her head fully out from under the red hanky and looked up with dark marble eyes to see the four faces hovering over her.

"She's not very old," Zack said. "She was born in the section shed out behind the train. Some of the workers found her while they were cleaning out the shed and fixing it up. She got separated from her mother some way and they saved her. Her name is Hudson, like in the name of the Railroad. There was another kitten, too. They named her Delaware. But she didn't make it."

"That's so sad," said Jackie.

"Hey, let me hold Hudson a minute," said Justin. He took off his black bucket hat and held it upside-down like a cloth bowl. Zack carefully transferred the kitten from his engineer cap into the bucket hat. Justin gently touched her tiny head. "Her face isn't even as big around as the face on my watch!" he said.

"Maybe it's a good thing Dax didn't come," said Jackie. "She might get jealous!"

There was only one thing Justin loved more than cats. Well, not really.

The horn sounded and the train lurched forward. The sudden movement kicked in all their senses. There were scraping and banging sounds and a slight smell of smoke and oil lingering in the air.

"Here we go," said Zack, talking louder now over the noise of the moving train. For a moment it looked out the window like the station was moving instead of the train. "The payroll isn't robbed until we are on our way back," he said.

"Then we'll spend our money at the ice-cream caboose at the Riverside Station in Raparius before the robber gets it," said Justin. "Chocolate with chocolate sprinkles," he said. "I can taste it now."

"Yipee," said Nick, without any enthusiasm. He rested his popcorn bag on his lap and laid his head back into his chair. "Just let me know when we get there," he said, and closed his eyes.

Bang-bang-bang-bang-bang-bang-bang-bang. The sound of tree branches slapping against the side of the train as it chugged forward sounded like the rapid fire of gunshots.

Nick sat up. "Is it happening already?" he asked.

Jackie laughed. "What's the matter, Nick?" she asked. "A little more nervous than you thought?"

CHAPTER III

Robbed!

"Welcome aboard the Upper Hudson River Railroad," the conductor announced over the train's speaker system. "Please pay attention. We have an important announcement to make."

"That's your cousin's dad talking now, right?" asked Jackie.

Justin nodded. He was still totally absorbed with Hudson and reluctantly handed the kitten back to Zack for safekeeping.

The conductor continued. "This afternoon the train is carrying a strongbox with a large payroll. We have just received a Western Union telegram and have been asked by the local sheriff to be on the lookout for several outlaws that have been spotted in the area. We understand they are armed and dangerous."

"Are we there yet?" asked Nick.

"We're only about halfway there," said Zack.

Jackie pointed out toward the Hudson River that flowed right alongside the train. "Enjoy the view," she said. The train slightly jerked and rocked. "Oh, no!" She stood and leaned forward with her hands

The outlaw stared at Justin through eyes
that were as black as his hat...

pressed against the window glass and there was panic in her voice. "We're falling into the river!"

Nick sat up quickly and looked out the window. It appeared there was nothing beneath the train but water. The car rocked and squealed again. "We're goners!" he said, and screamed.

Jackie dropped back into her chair and laughed out loud. "It was just a bridge," she said, and then crossed her arms and smiled. "Got you back."

"Very funny," said Nick. His popcorn was still in his lap, but outside the bag. He began to pick up the pieces one by one and drop them back into the paper container.

Jackie was still laughing. "Don't forget the ones on the floor," she said.

The train jerked one more time, but this time it came to a complete stop. The brakes scraped and screeched and then it was quiet. Very quiet. Passengers were looking back and forth out their windows.

"It's him! It's him! It's the robber!" The excited voice of a young child from the back end of the coach broke the silence.

Justin leaned out on the arm of his chair and looked down the long narrow aisle.

A man wearing a large cowboy hat had just entered car number three and was slowly making his way toward them.

"Stop in the name of the law," the youngster yelled.

"Somebody get the sheriff," yelled another.

13

As the thief made his way down the aisle grunting commands at passengers, a little boy broke the rules. He jumped out of his chair and began chasing him. "Come back with my daddy's money!" he wailed.

People continued to laugh and place things into the robber's bag as he worked his way from chair to chair. Justin turned to sit back fully in his seat. "He's getting closer," he said. "And he's sure getting a lot of loot."

Zack looked confused. "This is all wrong," he said. "The train never stops here." He stood up. "This must be something new. Watch Hudson for me. I'm going to go check with Dad."

Before Justin or Jackie or Nick could say a word, Zack bolted out of his seat and disappeared up the aisle away from the thief toward the forward cars and engine.

Justin could see the brim of the robber's hat hovering in the aisle above Nick's seat. He kept telling himself the robbery wasn't real, but he couldn't help it – he was still nervous.

Then it was their turn. "All right, kids, put your most valuable possessions right here in this bag." He thrust the pouch-shaped leather bag toward Justin with gloved hands and stared at him through eyes that were as black as his hat and the bandanna that covered the bottom half of his face. "Give until it hurts, so you don't have to!"

"I don't have very much money," said Justin, weakly. He pulled out his pocket watch and a few coins he was saving for ice cream. "This is all I have." He held out the coins.

"This will do," said the thief. He snapped the watch from Justin's grasp and dropped it into the bag. Then he looked at Nick. "Now what about you?"

"Would you like some popcorn?" Nick asked. He held up the paper bag and grinned.

"So you're a wise guy," said the robber, and reached out toward him suddenly with his free arm. Startled, all three Adirondack kids closed their eyes.

Jackie was the first one who dared to look again. "He's gone," she said. "Boy, that was sure different from the way they do the robberies on the Scenic Railroad back at camp."

"I guess he did want the popcorn," said Nick, searching the floor at his feet for the missing bag. He looked at Justin. "That was weird the way he just grabbed your watch like that."

Justin was frowning. He leaned out and looked again back up the aisle. "That guy had better get back here with it quick," he said.

Jackie tapped his shoulder. "I don't think he's coming back right away," she said. Justin turned and she gestured outside.

Now everyone was looking and pointing out the windows on the side of the train opposite the river. There was the bandit on a horse, galloping for the trees. Just before the horse and rider were about to disappear, a low-hanging branch caught the masked man across the chest and brought him crashing to the ground.

Everyone watching groaned.

Then he stood and limped off after the horse. Still clutching his bag, he vanished into the woods.

Everyone watching cheered.

"Can I have your attention, please?" It was the conductor, standing at the end of the car trying to raise his voice above the noise of the excited crowd. Zack stood alongside him. "We need everyone to remain calm and in their seats," he said. "Ladies and gentlemen." He cleared his throat. "The Upper Hudson River Railroad has just been robbed."

There was spontaneous applause.

"That was wonderful," said one passenger.

"It was so real," said another.

"Please, please," the conductor said soberly, motioning with uplifted hands for quiet. Everyone could sense slight tension in the air; and for just a moment, he had everyone's undivided attention. The only sound was the low hum of the train's idling engine. He spoke slowly and deliberately once again. "Ladies and gentlemen, this is very serious. The train *has* just been *robbed*."

CHAPTER IV

Catnapped

As the train sat waiting for the authorities to arrive, Justin sat stunned. The pocket watch given to him by his grandfather had been swiped. Safe for years with his great grandfather and years with his grandfather, in his hands it was lost within hours. "I can't believe this is happening," Justin said. "Grandpa's watch is gone."

"I can't believe you showed it to him," said Nick. "All I gave him was some popcorn."

Jackie interrupted. "It's not your fault, Justin," she said. "A lot of people were robbed on the train."

"I'll say," said Zack, who jumped back into his seat to rejoin his cousin and new friends. "People gave the bandit all kinds of stuff. I heard the sheriff tell Dad he got lots of jewelry and even some wallets."

"Hey, where were the sheriff and the deputies, anyway?" asked Justin. "Why weren't they doing their job?"

"They were," said Zack. "A couple of them went outside to check on the tree that was cut down, blocking the train. I found Dad helping the sheriff,

17

handing out Wanted Posters in the second car. That's why the bad guy took off. They were on their way."

"So he didn't rob everybody?" asked Jackie.

"Nope," said Zack. "After robbing our car, he took off."

"It figures," said Justin.

"Hey, where's my cap?" asked Zack.

"I don't know," said Justin. "It should be right on the seat where you left it."

Zack shifted and felt all around his body on the seat. Nothing. He got down on his hands and knees to search the floor.

"Are you sure you didn't take it with you when you went to talk to your dad?" asked Jackie.

"No," said Zack. He began breathing rapidly. "I am positive I left it right here."

"The robber must have taken the cap, too," said Jackie.

Zack sounded desperate. "But if he took my cap it means – "

Justin finished the awful sentence. "It means he also took Hudson."

CHAPTER V

25-Cent Museum

Justin woke up with a smile. But then he remembered. He wasn't in his own bed in Eagle Bay. He was at his cousin's house in North Creek. And his pocket watch was gone. Dax purred in his face and he remembered something else. Zack's kitten was gone, too. Somehow that bothered him even more than losing the family heirloom.

Justin got dressed quickly and headed out to the kitchen where Jackie, Nick and Zack were already eating breakfast and talking about the robbery.

"There is nothing you can do about it right now, Zachary," Mrs. Casey said. "Your father is still helping out at the station." She poured her son a second tall glass of orange juice. "The police are doing everything they can to find Hudson and everyone's stolen belongings. Why don't you show Justin and his friends your museum this morning? It will help take your mind off things."

"Can we sleep in the loft tonight?" asked Zack.

"I don't see why not," his mom said.

"So show us," said Jackie. "Justin said you have

Jackie turned and put her hands
on her hips. "Very funny," she said.

a lot of strange things in there. I'd like to see them."

"And Jackie is not afraid of anything," Justin said, "except spiders."

Zack nodded. "Really?" he said, and chugged down his orange juice. His eyes brightened. "All right, let's go."

The four friends dashed out the door toward the barn. The large wooden structure was made of rough-cut lumber and stood by itself out in the spacious yard. It was tall and wide and stained chocolate brown. Larger than the house, its slightly sagging peak repeated the blunted pattern of the mountain tops that lay beyond the roofline on the horizon. Jackie's long legs carried her to the barn door first.

"Go ahead and open it," called Zack, as he and the boys raced to catch up to her.

Jackie lifted the large wooden latch and grabbed the handle of the oversized door. Due to the loose top hinge, the bottom of the weathered door scraped across the ground as she pulled to swing it open. She turned to enter the structure and stopped short. A large black bear standing on its hind legs towered over her – with claws extended and teeth bared. She froze.

And then she realized the bear was frozen, too.

Frozen stiff.

Zack began to laugh. "He's stuffed," he said, but talked like the bear was very much alive. "Justin, Nick, Jackie – meet Lucky."

Jackie turned and put her hands on her hips. "Very funny."

"I didn't know anything about it," said Justin.

Nick looked up at the giant creature. "He sure doesn't look lucky," he said.

Zack brushed past Jackie and the eight-foot bear. He emerged with a crude sandwich sign that he propped on the ground facing the road.

Zack's Museum of Natural History, the sign said.

The bear stood on a platform with wheels. "He's pretty heavy," Zack said. "But he moves easy this way." Zack rolled the bear out of the barn and positioned it behind the sign. "That always gets people's attention."

Jackie started back into the barn and stopped again. She looked at Justin. "Um, you can go ahead," she said.

Justin paused.

"Come on you guys," said Nick. He pushed Justin aside. "How are we going to sleep in here tonight, if nobody will even go in during the day? It's just a funny animal museum, not a haunted house." He shook his head. "Chickens." He walked into the barn's wide, open mouth. Before the others could follow, he yelled, and ran back out.

"What's wrong?" Justin asked.

"Something grabbed my head," said Nick.

The three guests turned to face Zack. He shrugged his shoulders. "It was probably the owl," he said.

This time they all let Zack lead the way. Shafts of morning light poured in through several windows and small cracks and holes in the barn wall, but it was still fairly dark inside. Sinister looking shapes could be made out here and there in the dim light. Zack felt along the wall just inside the door and flipped a large metal switch. A fat single bulb hanging from a beam high above illuminated the large open building, casting plenty of light on now familiar creatures. A Barred Owl with outspread wings was likewise suspended from the ceiling, but hung by a thick rope a few feet from the floor. It was still slightly swinging.

Nick rubbed the top of his head. "So, it *was* a bird that got me."

"Wow," said Justin, as he gazed around the room. "My mom and dad said you had a lot of cool stuff, but this is awesome."

The bear at the entrance and the owl above were only the beginning. There were real preserved mammals in natural poses all about the cavernous room including a fisher and bobcat, an ermine and opossum. There were also snake skins, bees nests and turtle shells. A large glass case on the wall contained butterflies, moths, beetles and spiders.

The wood plank floor creaked beneath Justin's feet as he walked over to check out the fisher. "This is kind of cool and creepy all at the same time," he said, and looked down at a snarling coyote. "You must have every animal in the Adirondacks in here."

"Not quite," said Zack. "Actually, we only have a few of them."

"But none of the animals in here are breathing,"

said Nick. He was admiring a row of labeled skulls that were lined up at eye level on a counter near the entrance. "Here's a raccoon." He chuckled. "I mean, here *was* a raccoon," he said. "Poor thing." There was also the skull of a skunk. "Do the bones smell?" Nick leaned down to sniff it, but pulled back quickly. The skull of a beaver sat right beside the skunk skull, with jaws open wide. A small sign next to it read, **Museum Donation – 25 Cents**.

"I bought a pair of downhill skis for Gore Mountain with what I made last year," Zack explained. "My mom said I could earn a lot more if I didn't make people put the money inside the beaver's mouth. I guess its those front teeth that look like fangs that keep people from paying."

"Where did you get all these animals?" asked Jackie as she moved quickly past the case containing butterflies, moths and – spiders.

"My grandpa was a taxidermist," Zack said.

"So he bought all these things with the money he collected?" asked Nick. "I would have bought some new video games."

Jackie shook her head. "A taxidermist doesn't collect tax money," she said. "It is somebody who is really good at stuffing animals."

"Right," said Zack. "Grandpa did a lot of things for a living. He cut lumber and worked for a while at the garnet mines. I got the idea for the museum after hearing some neat stuff at school about President

Roosevelt. When he was young, he found the skull of a seal and started a museum like this in his own bedroom. But his parents made him move it."

"I vote this is our new clubhouse," said Nick.

"Every time we find a great new place, you want to make it a new clubhouse," said Jackie. "Pioneer Village in the woods back home will always be our official headquarters."

"So what," said Nick. "We should have clubhouses all over the Adirondacks."

"It's all right with me," said Zack.

"Whatever," said Jackie.

Justin was admiring some old snowshoes hanging on the wall. "These are pretty cool," he said.

"My grandpa gave me those," said Zack. "They are kind of like an inheritance."

Justin reached into his empty pockets. It reminded him of his lost watch. "I vote we go to the village and see if anybody's heard anything about the robber," he said.

Dax walked in and looked up cautiously at the owl hanging above her. She purred and Zack looked over at her cuddling up to Justin's leg. It made him think of the lost kitten.

"And I vote we go see if anybody's heard anything about Hudson," said Zack.

Nick nodded. "We can ask people questions and search for clues," he said.

"You're not the Hardy Boys," said Jackie, as she followed Dax and the boys out of the museum.

A sign that said, **CLOSED**, dangled from the neck of the bear on the wheels as the three aspiring boy detectives, a reluctant girl and a calico cat broke from a trot into a run toward the village.

CHAPTER VI

Horsing Around

"Wait up," Nick said. He was panting heavily. "I'm out of breath."

As Justin, Zack, Jackie and Dax waited at the top of the hill by the bank, a boy on a skateboard came straight at them from the church across the street. He bent his knees slightly and then kickflipped the curb where they stood, landed solidly on all four wheels and then tipping the board back onto its tail, skidded and stopped on the cement inches from them. Nick finally caught up to the group.

"Wassup, dude?" asked the skater. He and Zack grabbed right hands, slapped palms and punched fists.

"Not much," said Zack. He turned to the others. "This is Ryan," he said. "He's a senior at our school and the best skater in town."

"Have you heard anything more about the train robbery?" asked Justin.

"Nothing new," the skater said, adjusting his long baggy jeans. "There were some TV people down at the station early this morning. It's all a pretty big deal."

"Did you get another new skateboard?" asked Zack.

There was Dax, sitting calmly on the skateboard
in front of the North Creek Market Place.

"Yeah, it's awesome, too," said Ryan. "Check out the graphics on the bottom of the deck." He reached down for his board. "Hey, where did it go?"

"Dax!" said Jackie. Everyone turned.

The calico was off – four furry legs planted on a board with four wheels headed down the steep hill toward the center of busy Main Street.

"Those wheels are loaded with Abec 7's!" said Ryan. He took off after her. Justin was already on his way.

"What does 'Abec 7' mean?" asked Jackie, as she and Nick joined in the pursuit.

Zack was right alongside them. "It means she is going really fast and really far!" he said.

Dax was having fun. At least it looked like she was. Her whiskers bent back slightly in the breeze as she gained momentum and sped past the floral shop and the hardware store toward a street corner.

"No!" cried Justin, as the skateboard left the corner curb, rocketed through midair and crashed back to the ground.

Dax held on like a pro. The board skidded slightly, avoided the next curb and veered out into the street toward the rear end of a huge soda truck that was parked in front of the bakery.

"No..." said Justin again, this time faintly. He finally stopped, bent over and grabbed the bottom of his shorts, gasping for air.

Dax calmly laid down on the skateboard and easily cleared the rear bumper. The cat and the board flew underneath the soda truck and disappeared from view.

Half walking and half trotting, the remainder of the short walk to the middle of the village seemed to take forever. At least for Justin. He lost his watch. He wasn't going to lose Dax.

And Ryan wasn't about to lose his new skateboard. "I see the cat," he said. Justin's heart leaped and he discovered new energy to run on.

There she was, sitting on the board and calmly licking her front paws next to the ice-cream cone sign on the sidewalk in front of the North Creek Market Place.

Justin grabbed Dax off the board and squeezed her.

"Meow," said Dax. She peered over Justin's arms at the skateboard and reached out with her right paw.

"That was wicked great," said Ryan. "She acts like she wants to ride again." He reached out to shake hands with Justin, who did the best he could to repeat the strange combination of grabbing and slapping and punching of palms, fingers and fists. "Tell Zack I had to go." He threw his board underneath his feet and jumped on it all in a single motion. "Later, dawg," he said, as he zoomed off. "And cat!"

Justin waved and looked back up the street. *Where are those guys, anyway?* he thought. They were still moving toward him, but slowly. And they were looking at something and motioning out toward the street. Whatever it was, it had everyone's attention now. Cars were pulling over and people were moving out along the edge of the sidewalk like they were lining up to watch a parade.

"Look, Justin, look," called Jackie, as they approached him. Several cars were in his way, so he moved with everyone else out toward the curb.

It was a horse. Saddled and without a rider. And walking lazily right along the double yellow line in the middle of the street.

Jackie, Nick and Zack joined Justin in front of the deli just as the horse passed by. Its head bobbed and hooves clicked on the pavement in a slow and easy rhythm.

"It looks just like, Star," said Zack. "She's the only horse around here with a mark like that in the center of her forehead. She belongs to Miss Hawkins up on the River Road."

"Something just dropped out of the stirrup onto the pavement next to her," said Jackie.

Zack bolted out into the road, grabbed the object and hurried back.

"What is it?" asked Justin.

Zack held it up while still catching his breath. "It's a cowboy boot."

CHAPTER VII

Read All About It!

"EXTRA – EXTRA – READ ALL ABOUT IT!" Someone from the local newspaper pushed through the crowd along the street and was waving a small stack of papers over his head.

All the yelling and waving achieved the desired effect, as people followed the young man to the newspaper rack located in the shadow of the Market Place's blue awning. Justin was one of them.

The *News-Enterprise* usually came out once a week, but the robbery called for a special edition. Justin picked a copy up. It was 75 cents. He reached into his pocket and pulled out the coins the robber had left behind, the coins he was going to spend on an ice-cream cone. And they did serve ice cream just inside at the counter.

He looked at the headline on the front page of the newspaper above the fold. It was all about the robbery. Right next to the main story, there was a huge full-color photograph of the conductor talking to the police at the train station.

Zack's dad on the front page of the newspaper!

Justin thought. *Wait until everybody sees this!* That left no question as to where the 75 cents in his pocket was going today. He rushed in to buy the paper and ran back out to show it to Zack and his friends.

"I vote we read it right now," said Justin. It was unanimous.

They hurried along Main Street to the North Creek Depot, taking a shortcut down a steep sloping hill that emptied into the station's parking lot. Racing up onto the platform, they chose a bench in the shade near the front door of the museum.

Zack noticed one of the railroad's hired hands with a paintbrush walking along the platform. The man suddenly stopped and looked toward the footwear in his hand. Zack shoved the cowboy boot behind him to hide it from view.

Dax dodged people who were passing back and forth in and out of the museum and sought shelter under the seat at their feet.

"Read the story out loud," said Zack.

Nick agreed. "We've already got a boot," he said. "Maybe we'll find some more clues." He noticed even Jackie looked interested. "Hey remember now, we're not the Hardy Boys and so you're not Sammy Keyes."

"Ha, ha," Jackie said, flatly. "Go ahead, Justin, read."

Justin held the newspaper while the others squeezed in to look over his shoulders. The entire edition was filled with photographs and interviews and even special articles about local robberies from the past. There was also an editorial from the publisher.

Justin cleared his throat and began to read the main story on the front page, beginning with the headline.

Upper Hudson River Railroad Robbed – Bandit Still at Large

by SHANE DeKAMP
News-Enterprise Correspondent

NORTH CREEK – State Police have joined local law enforcement officers in the search for a man who robbed the Upper Hudson River Railroad on Friday afternoon during the train's regular eight-and-a-half mile run from the North Creek Railroad Depot to Raparius.

Officers said they believe the thief, who felled a tree on the tracks in order to stop and board the train which was filled to capacity with 350 passengers, was probably acting alone and could by now be miles away.

"We are looking for an unshaven white male, about 6 feet tall," said

Deputy Harris, the officer in charge. "He was last seen wearing black pants, black gloves, a black vest, a black cowboy hat and a black mask. We don't think he was armed, but we still consider him to be dangerous," the deputy said.

Police would not say how much money the thief got away with, but it is known that he jumped onto the caboose and robbed passenger cars five, four and three before his presence was discovered by an alert young rider whose name was not released for reasons of safety. Passengers said the thief then left the train and mounted a horse, finally disappearing into the woods.

"We are glad everyone on the train was unharmed," said long-time conductor, Mike Casey, of North Creek. "We are working with the police around the clock to see this crime is solved."

Casey also said the special reenactment of Theodore Roosevelt's dash for the Presidency scheduled for Sunday at the North Creek Depot will still be held.

(Story continued on page four)

Nick looked at Zack. "Wow. You're a hero," he said. "It's too bad no one knows your name."

"They didn't say anything at all about Hudson," said Zack. "It's like no one even cares."

Justin put his arm on his cousin's shoulder. "Well, *we* care," he said. "And we aren't going to stop searching until we find her."

"Aren't you forgetting something?" said Jackie. They all looked at her. "We are only here one more day. Tomorrow night, we go home."

CHAPTER VIII

Riding the Bubble

Saturday was slipping away fast. The Adirondack kids had been all over the village probing for more information about the robbery, but without any more luck.

Everyone recalled the bank robbery that had occurred not long ago. But North Creek was a quiet, peaceful hamlet. Most of the stories they heard were about robberies past, as local memories were stirred by the special edition of the *News-Enterprise*. There was the stagecoach robbery a hundred years ago in nearby North River; and in the early 1900's a thief was caught robbing local stores.

"The business owners all formed their own posse," they heard one gray-haired man say at the Café Sarah. "The crook came out of the old Smith's store one night and nearly the whole town was outside waiting for him!"

The four friends took turns carrying the boot which they continued to hide wrapped up in their newspaper; and Justin spent much of the day keeping track of Dax who kept disappearing to explore her new surroundings.

Zack looked up at the clock on the corner of the Village Square. "It's 5:30," he said. "I've got one more idea. Follow me." He led the young posse of his own back down to the station, but this time beyond the tracks to the old section shed where Hudson was first found. "Maybe we can find some clues around here." The outside of the renovated building still smelled of fresh paint.

Jackie looked a little uncomfortable. "Should we even be around these buildings without permission?" she said. "I vote we go back to Zack's house and look again tomorrow."

"But tomorrow will be too late," argued Zack. "You said you would keep helping until we found Hudson."

"Dax, come back here," said Justin. The curious calico had slipped away again, this time through the tall green grass leading away from the buildings and train tracks toward the riverbank. He sighed and took off after her.

"You guys can stay here and argue some more if you want to, but I am getting kind of hungry," said Nick. "I vote with Jackie." Then he ran after Justin along the thin trail that snaked its way through the vegetation that grew taller and more dense as he moved closer to the river.

Justin could hear the moving Hudson River just ahead. "Where are you, girl?" he said, and parted the last of the grass in front of him with his hands. There sat Dax in the middle of a small gray rubber raft hidden in a thick green blanket of weeds at the edge of the water. "I know you love boats, but this one isn't ours. Come on out of there." She backed away as he reached out for her. "Come on, Dax." Carefully he stepped into the raft and reached out for her again.

"Hey, where are you guys?" It was Nick, and he was moving fast.

"Be careful, Nick," said Justin. "We're over –"

Before Justin could say, "here," Nick exploded through the vegetation and was upon them. His foot stuck in the mud and he stumbled forward through the air, spilling into the boat and forcing the small craft out into the river.

Jackie and Zack finally appeared at the shore and were shocked to find their friends floating in the water.

Justin and Nick were both reaching out over the edges of the small boat, trying to use their arms as oars to move back to shore. "Help us," said Justin. "There aren't any paddles in here." The water was fairly calm, but the boat was still starting to slowly drift away.

Jackie and Zack began searching frantically in the weeds.

"Got one," said Jackie. She held the paddle out with one of her long arms, but it kept falling short, the wide flat end slapping on the water surface just beyond Justin's outstretched arm.

"Jump out," said Zack. "The water isn't that deep. Hurry before you get out much further."

Justin and Nick looked down into the water. They

could see the bottom, but they were still nervous.

"Well, maybe," said Justin.

"Good," said Jackie. "That's a maybe and a maybe is –"

Before she could say, "yes", the water suddenly began to rise and the boat lifted on a series of waves that washed all around and under it.

"What's happening?" yelled Justin. "What's happening?"

"You're on the bubble!" cried Zack. "You're riding on the bubble!"

"What's the bubble?" asked Jackie.

"It's a special water release from up the river," explained Zack. "It can make the river rise a foot or more."

The two stood stunned on the shore – Jackie holding a paddle and Zack holding the cowboy boot wrapped in the newspaper. The river, so calm moments before, was now a foamy torrent. They watched helplessly as the small rubber raft carrying Justin, Nick and Dax bobbed and swirled madly about and was furiously swept away.

CHAPTER IX

Down the Hudson River

Justin and Nick watched as Jackie and Zack grew smaller and smaller and then disappeared. Without any way to steer, they were at the mercy of the river. It seemed whenever they tried to sit up to gain their balance, the raft would spin and send them back to the bottom of the boat.

"Here Nick, put this on," Justin said. He handed his friend one of two life jackets that were aboard. It was a struggle, but they both finally managed to don a lifesaving device. Justin grabbed Dax with one arm. He didn't want her holding onto the rubber raft with her claws. With Dax under control, he pulled himself up enough to peer over the side of the runaway raft.

It was the middle of July, and the water level was still rather low. It was just deep enough to keep rushing them along, but not deep enough to cover the tops of all the rocks and boulders that littered the liquid pathway up ahead.

"What are we going to do?" asked Nick. His eyes and cheeks were wet – not with spray – with tears.

Without any way to steer, Justin and Nick
were at the mercy of the river.

"We'll just have to ride it out," said Justin. "We can do it, Nick. We've been in the putt putt at camp in rough water a lot worse than this."

They heard the train whistle and looked up. There was Locomotive No. 5019 high above them, faithfully pulling its five passenger cars and caboose on a special private party run alongside the river.

"Help, help!" Justin and Nick started yelling and waving excitedly in an effort to gain attention and rescue.

The people on the open-air caboose waved back. So did some people sitting in the coaches. And then the entire train was swallowed up by a large stand of trees.

"Do you think they'll send help?" asked Nick.

Justin thought the people were just being friendly, but he didn't want to discourage his friend. "Maybe," he said.

The two boys shifted to look down the river again.

"That's awfully big to be a rock," said Nick.

Justin saw it, too. A tall thin object rose above the waterline, higher than anything else around it.

"It's moving," said Nick.

The raft moved in closer.

"It's a person," said Justin.

The raft moved closer.

"It's a fisherman," said Nick.

The angler seemed as surprised to see them as they were to see him. The unruly motion of the boat made it impossible for the man in waders to decide which direction to go to get out of the way. The sudden rise in the water level caught him off guard as well.

"Help!" cried Nick as they swept by, missing the fisherman by only a few feet. As if by instinct, he reached out for the fishing line and caught it. The end of the line appeared quickly and the hook became lodged in the side of the boat. They could feel a slight jerk and then watched as the man's pole suddenly flew from his hands. Their last look at him was of waving fists.

"I don't know about the people on the train, but I'll bet you that guy comes looking for us," said Justin.

"Here come the rocks," said Nick.

"Hang on," said Justin.

The gray raft missed the first few, but finally glanced off a small boulder, bouncing away from it sideways. Then they hit another. And another. Each time they bounced off in another direction, like a silver ball in a pinball machine. Once or twice they felt a rock that was hidden just below the water surface push up on the flimsy floor underneath them.

As usual, Dax appeared to be having fun. Justin knew how fearless she was, and held her again so her small body would not be jarred overboard and into the churning foam.

The last bounce careened the craft as close to the side of the river as they had been since the whole unintentional journey had begun. The water was deeper there, but much more calm. It was like coasting the last few feet at the end of a wild ride at an amusement park. An easy current carried them to the trunk of an uprooted birch tree that stretched from the bank out into the water.

Justin grabbed for a branch. "I got it," he said.

Nick joined him in using the limbs to pull the raft to shore. They tumbled out and pulled it fully out of the water, glad to have their feet on dry ground again. They unsnapped their life jackets and tossed them into the boat.

"What time is it?" Nick asked.

"I have no idea," said Justin. The sun was still bright, but low in the sky. It had not occurred to him until right then to consider how much daylight they might have left to be found.

The train whistle sounded again, but from very far away.

"Maybe we can stand here and wait for the train to come back," suggested Nick.

That seemed like a good idea.

"But what if it is dark by then?" said Justin. "They won't be able to see us to stop."

Nick lowered his head. "We're doomed," he said. Looking down he noticed a pair of footprints in the mud. "Hey, look at these."

Justin looked down. "That's funny," he said. "Look at how different they are. It's like there was a shoe on one foot and the other foot was bare. You can even see the toes."

"Who would be out in the middle of nowhere walking around with just one shoe on?" asked Nick and laughed.

Justin thought, and his own smile disappeared. "Maybe the print is not from a shoe," he said.

"What do you mean?" asked Nick.

Justin spoke more softly as he studied the distinct impression in the mucky ground. "Maybe it's from a boot," he said, and looked around nervously.

Understanding waxed across Nick's face. "You mean like a *cowboy* boot?" he asked.

Justin nodded.

CHAPTER X

Crook in the Creek

Nick followed Justin and Dax up the steep bank. The only sounds now were from the rushing water of the Hudson River below them and their own heavy breathing. They reached the train tracks above and began to run on top of the narrow steel rails back toward North Creek, like daring tightrope walkers in a circus barely maintaining their balance. But they knew that was dangerous and felt too exposed up so high, anyway. They hurried down the grassy bank on the side of the tracks near the edge of the woods.

Justin motioned them forward and hadn't moved more than a few feet when he stopped abruptly.

"What is it?" Nick said.

Justin pointed at the ground. It was a small red rubber raft, partially covered by leaves and broken branches.

Dax jumped up onto the side of the boat and began to lose her balance on its smooth rounded edge. She dug in with her claws for a firm grip. "Dax, no," said Justin. He reached out for her and tugged, but she hung on stubbornly.

There was an odd crunching sound in the woods and the two boys squatted quickly. Dax's determined grip finally came free with Justin's sudden movement toward the ground.

"Maybe it's just a camper or a fisherman who can help us," whispered Nick.

Justin shrugged. "Maybe," he said. "But let's be quiet – just in case."

"Just in case of what?" Nick asked.

"You know, in case it *is* the bad guy," said Justin. He carried Dax, which was especially awkward with the way they chose to move ahead. The two boys remained in a crouched position, and slowly advanced into the forest, waddling like penguins. The earth was soft and moist under their feet. The air in the slight dampness smelled somehow sweet and sour at the same time.

"It hurts my legs to walk this way," complained Nick.

"Shhh!" said Justin. He pointed toward their knees. "Be careful stepping over this barbed-wire fence."

The two boys managed to clear the fence without incident, and as they waddled closer to the mysterious sound they could now hear each crunch was followed by a low thump.

Justin continued to lead and could make out the shape of a man in the black shade of the tall leafy trees that towered all around them. The man's head was down, and it appeared he was hard at work with a shovel in his hands.

"I can see somebody," whispered Justin. "I think there's a lean-to behind him." The crude structure was located at the bottom of a steep, tree-littered ridge that rose like a wall directly behind it.

"So he *is* camping," said Nick. "What's making that sound?"

"He's digging a hole," said Justin.

"What for?" asked Nick.

"I don't know," said Justin. "Let's get closer."

Leafy vegetation now covered the forest floor. The boys kept low and finally crawled for shelter behind a small boulder. They sat down behind the welcomed cover and stretched their legs out in front of them.

Nick groaned. "My legs are getting cramps," he said. "I sure hope we don't have to run."

The shoveling sound stopped. There was an eerie quiet.

What if he's moving toward us right now? Justin thought.

"What do you think he's doing?" whispered Nick.

"I'll take a look," said Justin. Still hanging on to Dax, he used his one free hand for stability and slowly pulled himself up to peer over the top of the boulder. His black bucket hat helped the top of his head blend in with their dark surroundings.

"I don't see him," said Justin. The man reappeared from behind the lean-to. "Wait, there he is." Justin couldn't see his face, but he didn't have to. The man was wearing a black cowboy hat, a black vest and was carrying a small leather bag.

The man was wearing a black cowboy hat,
a black vest and was carrying a small leather bag.

Justin lowered his head and whispered to Nick. "This isn't a campsite. It's a hideout."

"No way," said Nick.

"Yes, way," said Justin. "It's him."

The two friends lifted their heads together to observe the thief at work.

"That's the bag your pocket watch is in," said Nick.

"That's the bag Hudson is in," said Justin.

They watched as the man took off his black vest and threw it into the freshly dug hole. Then he took off his gloves and threw them into the hole as well.

"There's something else in his hands," said Justin. A red handkerchief appeared and he wiped his sweaty brow.

"That's Zack's bandanna," said Justin.

"So where is Hudson?" said Nick. "Is she still in the bag?"

"She must be," said Justin. "I don't see her anywhere."

They were shocked to watch the man then throw the leather bag into the hole and step down on it hard with his left foot – the only foot that had a boot on it.

Justin couldn't believe it.

"Poor Hudson," said Nick.

They were helpless. The man was simply too big and too dangerous. He picked up the shovel and began filling in the hole.

"I wish he would turn around so we could see his face," said Justin.

"I can't kneel like this any more," said Nick. "My legs are killing me." He slipped back down and his knee landed on a dry stick. It snapped.

The man started to turn around. Justin's face flushed red as he dropped on the ground next to his friend.

"Who's there?" said the man. They could tell as the man continued to mumble he was moving closer. "Come on out." Justin could feel his cheeks burning. It sounded like the man was almost upon them.

Dax squirmed from Justin's grasp and scampered out into the open.

Justin whispered sternly. "Dax, no."

"Well, where did you come from, kitty, kitty?" The two boys could hear the man turning away from them. "Look at all those colors. You sure are a pretty thing. Come on back here."

The man didn't really sound mean – nothing like he did when he was robbing the train. But all Justin could imagine was the man scooping Dax up and dropping her into the hole – buried alive. He decided he didn't care how big or dangerous the man was. Poor Hudson was lost. Nothing was going to happen to Dax. He was about to stand up and confront the crook face-to-face when another sound came from the ridge, high above the lean-to.

It was the sound of galloping horses.

CHAPTER XI

A Close Call

"Maybe it's the sheriff," said Justin, hopefully.

"And his deputies," said Nick. They dared to peek back over the boulder.

The thief was ignoring Dax now and moving about nervously. He quickly shoveled some more dirt back into the hole.

The galloping stopped, and was replaced by the sound of voices. The man appeared to be panicking and finally fled through the woods back toward the river, mainly hopping on the foot with the boot and holding his hat in place with one hand and his shovel with the other. The boys heard a sharp cry and a deep groan and they guessed he had reached the barbed-wire fence.

"Let's go," said Nick. "Now's our chance."

Dax was already ahead of them prancing upward, toward the voices. Nick took off behind her. But Justin ran toward the thief's hideout.

"What are you doing?" said Nick. "He might come back."

"I'm not leaving Hudson behind," said Justin. He

dropped to his knees at the hole and quickly pawed the dark earth away from the bag.

"Justin!" said Nick. "Come on!"

"Got it!" said Justin and ran to join his friend.

They scrambled up the steep ridge using the roots of trees as handles to pull themselves upward, and pushed off small rocks at their feet to keep from slipping back downward. As they half ran, half crawled up the steep slope on all fours, their knees would occasionally strike the ground.

At the top on level land, they finally felt the freedom to cry out.

"Over here!" Nick shouted.

"Help us!" Justin said.

"Stay where you are. We're coming." It didn't sound like the sheriff and his deputies. It didn't even sound like adults. It wasn't. Two young girls walked toward them, holding the reins of their horses. "What's wrong?" asked one of the girls. "Are you guys lost?" They both laughed.

"Well, sort of," said Justin. He looked around and noticed a small yellow marker on a tree. They were on some kind of trail. "We need to get back to North Creek."

"Hi, my name is Margaret," said the shorter of the two girls. She pointed to her friend. "This is Meredith."

"We can get you back to North Creek all right," Meredith said. She pulled her long black hair away from her face. "It's not that far."

"If you're not afraid of horses," said Margaret.

Justin was looking past the girls and marveled at the huge animals standing directly behind them. Meredith's horse was plain brown, with white around its hooves. But it was Margaret's horse he couldn't stop staring at. It was colored and marked just like his cat. It was like looking at a giant Dax with a long nose and puffy tail.

"Tell them about the robber," said Nick.

The two girls looked at Justin. "Robber?" they said, together.

"Trust me," Justin said. "We need to get out of here, quick." He looked over his shoulder back down the steep slope. "We'll tell you about it in town. We promise."

Neither Margaret nor Meredith asked any more questions. They held their horses steady while Justin and Nick struggled to get up into the saddles. It was an especially difficult task for Justin. He had picked up Dax and was trying to hold her and the leather bag and climb into the saddle of the monster horse all at the same time. With his arms full, it was nearly impossible to gain any balance. His knee nearly touched his nose, just trying to lift his foot high enough for it to enter the stirrup. He groaned. "Maybe I'll just walk," he said.

"Just watch out for the poison ivy," said Meredith.

"Poison ivy?" said Nick. Just the mention of it made him begin to scratch his arms and legs.

Margaret smiled at Justin. "I'll hand you your cat," she said, and reached out for the calico.

"Thanks, but she doesn't really trust strangers," said Justin. Dax jumped into her arms. "Well, not usually."

Once the boys were on the horses, the two girls mounted with ease. Each carrying a reluctant passenger, they were around and off the grassy trail quickly, trotting along the quiet, narrow River Road headed back to North Creek.

Shadows were long by the time they reached the village. Justin was happy to slide down off the horse. He could feel the tenseness of Dax's body while holding her throughout the ride, and sensed her desire to jump off at the first opportunity. They hadn't been riding long, but long enough for the inside of his legs to hurt.

"So, tell us about the robber," said Margaret. "You promised."

"And what's inside that pouch?" said Meredith.

"Okay," Justin said. "You both know about the train robbery yesterday?" They nodded. He took a deep breath. "Well, Nick here and our friend Jackie and my cousin Zack and I were robbed on the train, and the thief took my pocket watch and Zack's kitten."

"He stole a kitten?" said Margaret. "That's awful."

"But we don't think the guy knew he took a kitten, because it was hiding in my cousin's cap that he stole," explained Justin. "So we tried to find clues about the robbery in town all day and we went down to the train depot and Nick and I ended up in a raft in the river, but we didn't have any paddles ..."

"And we were scared out of our minds," said Nick, in an attempt to add some drama.

"When we got out of the river we found some footprints," said Justin. "Then we heard a noise in the woods and we thought it might be a camper, but it wasn't. It was the robber."

"The train robber?" asked Margaret in disbelief.

"That's not possible," said Meredith. "The police said he was probably long gone."

"Well, we saw him," said Justin. "And he was digging a big hole in the ground and he put some of his robber clothes into it, and this bag." He held it up.

"Yeah," said Nick. "And when he heard your horses coming, he stopped burying stuff and ran like crazy through the woods."

"So what's in the bag?" asked Margaret.

Justin and Nick looked at each other.

"We're not exactly sure," said Justin.

"Well, let's find out," said Margaret. "Open it."

Justin held the leather bag out in front of him. The large pouch with a drawstring at the top hung suspended between his two hands like an oriole's nest at the end of a branch on a maple tree. "I don't think you girls should watch," he said.

"Do it," said Margaret.

"Okay," said Justin. He slowly reached into the bag.

Nick was the one who closed his eyes.

CHAPTER XII

The Cat's Out of The Bag

Justin gritted his teeth as he inched his hand downward. He knew Hudson didn't weigh very much. "I feel something," he said.

Nick opened his eyes. "What is it?"

"I think it's money," said Justin. He moved his hand around. "And there's some jewelry – like small beads off a necklace or something."

"Well, show us the money," said Nick.

"We want to see the jewelry," said Margaret.

"Just a minute," said Justin. "I want to see if my pocket watch is still in here." He concentrated and groped all around the bottom of the deep pouch. He suddenly stopped and turned pale.

"What is it?" asked Nick. "What's wrong?"

"There's something warm and gushy," said Justin.

"Poor Hudson," said Nick.

"Do you mean the kitten?" asked Meredith.

Justin nodded, and slowly pulled his hand out of the bag.

"Oh, gross," said Margaret.

"That's disgusting," echoed Meredith.

Nick started laughing. "Half of a banana – you thought a banana was Hudson?"

"You said, 'Hudson', not me," Justin said, defensively. He looked around for somewhere to put the brown mushy fruit that was loosely sticking between his fingers. Not finding a suitable place to dispose of it, he snapped his wrist and flicked it back into the bag.

"Why did you do that?" asked Nick. "At least get all the money out first."

"You're starting to make me sick," said Margaret.

Justin wiped his hand on the outside of the bag and reached back in. He collected all the paper he could feel and pulled out a handful.

"Candy wrappers," said Nick.

"Let me guess," said Margaret. "There's no jewelry, either. Right?"

Justin knelt on the sidewalk and tipped the bag slightly sideways. A dozen popcorn kernels rolled out onto the cement.

"Did the guy you saw in the woods rob a train, or a grocery store?" asked Margaret.

"It probably wasn't even the robber," said Meredith.

"It really was the robber," insisted Justin. Nick nodded vigorously in support of his friend. "He must have taken out the money and other stuff and then just used it for a garbage bag."

"Well, at least Hudson wasn't in there," said Nick. The banana and candy bar wrappers and popcorn reminded him of how hungry he was. Even the girls' initials reminded him of food – M & M. He couldn't remember ever having gone so long without a meal. He had broken his own main rule of the road: Always bring extra goodies in each pocket in case of a food shortage emergency. "Can we go home now?" he asked. "It's got to be supper time."

With lights flashing, a police car rolled up and stopped along the curb. An officer emerged from the vehicle and adjusted his hat as he approached them. He was so big, he seemed to block out everything else around from view.

"Are your names Justin Robert and Nick Barnes?" the officer said. He wasn't smiling.

CHAPTER XIII

Midnight Madness

Justin had never ridden in a police car before. Neither had Nick. They told the officer everything they had told Margaret and Meredith. They had not meant to end up in the river. And they were even more surprised to find the train robber in the woods.

The officer politely nodded as they shared their adventure. "I've never heard of a lean-to anywhere near the bluff, and I've lived around here most of my life," he said. As the car pulled into the Casey's driveway he assured the boys he would check the area in the morning. "You fellows gave a lot of people a pretty good scare today. Be careful."

It wasn't easy to convince Zack's mom and dad that they could still sleep overnight in the loft of the barn. In fact, they didn't. Zack and his neighborhood friends had ridden the bubble on inner tubes before, but unscheduled trips were unacceptable. And waiting nervously throughout the late afternoon for the police to call didn't help at all. Begging, pleading and Zack's puppy-dog eyes at the supper table only succeeded in securing a compromise. They could stay in the barn, but only until midnight.

The four Adirondack kids marched single file across the lawn with flashlights which were hardly necessary. The grass at their feet and the barn ahead were washed silver in the glimmer of a full summer moon. The night mountain air was crisp and clean.

Zack led the way. He opened the barn door and rolled Lucky off to one side. Justin, Jackie and Nick tried to avoid pointing their flashlights at any of the animals as they carefully made their way to the permanent wooden ladder located near the center of the barn.

They hadn't walked far when Zack shone his light on the new display he and Jackie had made earlier that day. It featured the train robber's boot. "This will draw some crowds," he boasted, and turned to Justin. "Mom told us to keep busy while we were waiting to hear if you and Nick were okay."

Justin shook his head. "I can't believe the police or hardly anybody believes we saw the real train robber," he said.

"Why don't you think that policeman believed you?" asked Jackie. "He took the bag and said he would check tomorrow."

"That's how I know he doesn't believe us," Justin said. "If he believed us, he would have sent a bunch of police looking for him right away."

They continued weaving their way around the animals that were posed in their aggressive stances on the museum floor. Justin made the mistake of pointing his beam downward at the head of a snarling bobcat. All he could see were its penetrating eyes and pointed fangs. Even the mid-July heat could not keep a slight shiver from running down his spine. He could almost feel the animal snapping at his ankles as he climbed quickly up the ladder.

Once in the loft, the four friends arranged their sleeping bags, forming a square.

"Okay, let's check our supplies," said Justin. They emptied their pockets of candy bars and comic books and playing cards and dumped it all on the floor between them. "The peanut butter cups are mine," Justin reminded them.

Zack positioned his flashlight so that the beam flooded their immediate area. "You can turn your lights off now and save the batteries," he urged.

After a few games of cards, Nick began making shadow creatures on the barn wall. He locked his thumbs and began waving his eight fingers in front of the flashlight. "Guess what this is," he said.

Jackie looked at the zany silhouette that was magnified on the wall in front of her. "It's an angel," she said.

"Nope," said Nick.

"A butterfly," said Zack.

"Wrong again," said Nick.

"A bat!" said Justin.

Nick shook his head no. "Give up?" he asked.

"It's a bat!" Justin insisted.

"Take it easy, Justin, we're only playing a game," said Jackie.

Justin pointed upward and sure enough, what looked like a small mouse with wings was darting about in and out of the light, casting its own fleeting shadows on the barn wall and ceiling all around them.

Nick finally saw the shadow and pulled his sleeping bag over his head. "There's millions of them," he cried.

"There's only one," said Zack, and calmly reached over and switched off his flashlight. "That should do it," he said in the dark. "The little guy will find a place to land now."

"I think it's midnight," said Nick. "It must be time for us to go in now."

"Shhh," said Zack. "What is that?"

"I don't hear anything," said Justin.

"I hear it, too," said Jackie.

"Hear what?" asked Justin. Even though it was dark, he closed his eyes tightly to concentrate even better.

Squeeek.

"I do hear it," said Justin. "It's underneath us."

They couldn't see each other in the blackness of the loft, but they could see the door below as it slowly opened letting moonlight pour in onto the floor. The silver light began to hit the stationary animals broadside one by one, each creature casting its own long distorted shadow.

The silhouette of a man stood fully in the doorway, his long shadow joining those of the animals stretching across the floor. It was a shadow wearing a cowboy hat.

"It's the robber," whispered Justin. "It's got to be."

The figure moved cautiously into the museum. He took a single careful step and still the floor moaned beneath him.

The Adirondack kids sat in silence and watched as the figure gained confidence and picked up some speed with each step.

Justin whispered to Zack, but Zack didn't answer. He looked back out over the edge of the loft and noticed moonlight flicker along the edge of the rope holding the Barred Owl. It was wiggling. Then the bird itself slowly began to ascend.

"Get ready to grab the owl," whispered Zack. He had used a rake to pull the rope over to him and now, hand-over-hand, was hauling the large bird of prey heavenward.

Justin carefully stood up and reached out for the owl. He couldn't quite secure it, and so inched his way even closer to the edge of the loft. He leaned out to grab a wing. "Got it," he whispered, but misjudged the weight of the creature and began to lose his balance.

"Get ready to let the owl fly," whispered Zack. "I'll say when."

Nick stepped forward to help Justin regain his balance, and now it was the upstairs floor that creaked.

A flashlight clicked on from below; and like a laser with pinpoint accuracy, the beam projected upward toward Justin. But it wasn't Justin's face that was illuminated.

It was the owl's.

"Now!" whispered Zack. "Let her fly now!"

Justin didn't have a choice. Despite Nick's efforts to help, he could feel himself falling forward into wide open black space. He hugged the owl and closed his eyes.

Bird and boy took off with a whoosh, gaining speed as they descended like Tarzan swooping down upon the unwelcome intruder. The stunned man let out a gasp as the owl punched his chest and sent him sprawling onto the floor. Justin absorbed the sudden blow and clung tenaciously to the owl on the rope, still suspended and now spinning in place.

The dazed intruder scrambled to his feet and stumbled forward in an attempt to exit the barn. But instead of escaping, he misjudged and ran headlong into the waiting arms of another creature off in the shadows right next to the door. An eight-foot giant grabbed the hapless man by the shirt with a sinister claw.

The two emerged from the darkness – the huge black bear on wheels still clinging to the panicked man's shoulder. For a moment, man and bear were whirling in small circles, dancing in the moonlight. The man was yelling now, and in an effort to break free managed only to tip the bear and bring it crashing down fully on top of him. The claws of the bear drove into the wooden floor like spikes.

The only parts of the man that could be seen now from underneath his captor's massive body were flailing arms and legs. He was pinned and went on kicking and struggling to get free.

Justin couldn't hold on any more. He dropped the four feet from the owl to floor. The bear cushioned his fall.

The man underneath groaned and pushed upward one more time.

Justin rolled off the bear and took refuge behind the snarling bobcat just as the man finally broke free from his furry prison and ran limping out of the barn.

Jackie, Nick and Zack hurried quickly down the ladder just as Mr. and Mrs. Casey hurried into the barn from the house. They were in their pajamas and Dax was with them.

"What in the world is all the noise out here?" asked Mr. Casey. He flipped on the barn light. Both of Zack's parents were surprised to see the bear lying facedown in the middle of the floor. "What happened to Lucky?" he asked.

Mrs. Casey looked up at the Barred Owl still slightly moving at the end of its rope. Feathers were missing and a wing was broken. Justin could tell by the look on her face she was at the end of her rope, too.

"All right, time to go in," she said.

Mr. Casey agreed. "It is already quarter past midnight," he said. "We'll talk about all this in the morning."

Jackie and Zack were standing next to their new museum display.

"Wait, Mom and Dad," said Zack. "It's gone."

"What's gone?" asked his parents.

"The cowboy boot," said Jackie.

"He must have taken it," said Justin.

Zack's parents looked confused. "Who took it?" they asked.

Nick shook his head. "It looks like the robber robbed his boot," he said.

CHAPTER XIV

History Repeats Itself

There was extra security at the train depot in the morning. Word was out the bandit was still in the area, but the reenactment of Theodore Roosevelt's historic ride to the Presidency was not about to be canceled. In fact, news of the train robbery and barn break-in only seemed to enlarge the crowd.

The police were not happy the kids had not let them know about the boot, but were happy to have a lead as to the thief's whereabouts. A flat red raft with some small curious punctures had been found floating along the Hudson River. And a few more items were found in the hole by the lean-to at the bluff. All the evidence backed up the stories told by the Adirondack kids.

"At least everyone believes us now," said Justin. He and Zack were out on the platform where more and more people were gathering for the arrival of the President. Jackie was with Nick in the depot gift shop to buy more popcorn. Dax was sitting near the train on the conductor's stool.

"It seems like we just got here, and it's already time to go," said Justin.

"I'm sorry you lost your pocket watch," said Zack.
Justin sighed. "I'm sorry you lost Hudson."

"I know," said Zack. "I'm sorry you lost your pocket watch."

Justin sighed. "I'm sorry you lost Hudson."

"I heard that," said Jackie. "This isn't a time to be sad." She was carrying extra bags of Nick's favorite treat and handed one to each of them. "The sun is out and we have the whole day to spend together," she said, "and we are going to meet the President of the United States."

"Big deal," said Nick, trotting up beside her. "He's not even going to shoot any buffalo."

Mr. Casey walked the length of the platform to join them. He was back in uniform and looked very sharp as a conductor in his trim blue suit with gold buttons and black-rimmed blue cap accented by two thin gold braids. "Are you all ready to meet the President?" he asked, and adjusted his red, white and blue tie. "I'll introduce you after he receives the telegram that lets him know he has become the President, and everyone gets settled on the train."

There was the sound of trotting horses in the parking lot.

"Here he comes," someone shouted, and the crowd shifted together almost as one body to the edge of the platform facing the village and all the action.

Justin couldn't see anything standing behind so many adults, but he could look back toward the conductor's stool that now sat alone on the platform. It was empty. "Where's Dax?"

Jackie, Nick and Zack didn't hear him. They were

being swallowed up by the crowd, inching their way forward between the adults for a look at Theodore Roosevelt who was arriving in a horse-drawn carriage – just like the one the real Theodore Roosevelt had been carried in to the North Creek Depot more than a hundred years earlier.

She's got to be right around here, thought Justin, and began calling for her as he walked down the platform behind the crowd and past the museum and gift shop.

And then he thought, *What if she climbed underneath the cars and the train begins to move?* He walked more quickly. "Here Daxy. Here, kitty, kitty."

He paused and thought some more. It hit him. *What if she is headed back toward the river?* He turned and raced with his popcorn back toward the front of the train.

Retracing his steps from the morning before, he rounded the locomotive and crossed the tracks. Starting past the section shed, he heard a noise. "Dax, is that you?" He put his ear against the door.

"Meow."

"I hear you, girl," he said. "I'm coming." The shed door slid open. He slowly entered and looked for a light.

"Meow."

"Where are you, Dax?" said Justin.

Then he heard a softer meow – more like a mew. "Hudson?"

It *was* Hudson. Dax stood over her like a sentry.

The shed light suddenly came on and the door shut behind him.

"Well, you finally found the little kitty." It was an unfamiliar and unfriendly voice.

Justin turned to face two men now blocking the closed door. The one with brown paint on his hands looked slightly familiar, but the other he was quite confident he knew. It looked like he hadn't slept in several days, because of course, he hadn't. He was unshaven, his pants were torn and there was something that was odd about him. He kept itching. Justin looked at the man's feet. Any uncertainty as to his identity was wiped away. He would recognize that footwear anywhere.

"What are we going to do now?" asked the man in the cowboy boots.

The man with the paint on his hands didn't say anything.

Justin could remember being scared before, like when he thought he was lost on Bald Mountain. But this was different. Somehow he knew this was serious. Very serious. "I just wanted my cat," he heard someone say faintly. Then he realized it was he himself who had spoken.

The man still didn't say anything. He just kept staring.

"What are we going to do now?" asked the man in the cowboy boots again.

"I don't know!" said his partner. "This has all gotten way out of hand."

Justin set down his bag of popcorn on the floor, and picked up Hudson. "Can we go now?" he asked, hopefully.

There were voices outside.

"Justin?" someone called.

It's Jackie, thought Justin. He felt a spark of hope.

"Daxy," called another.

That's Nick. Oh, how good those voices sounded. The spark of hope was fanned into a flame.

"They're only kids, let's just run for it and get out of here," said the man with the cowboy boots.

The man with the painted hands didn't say anything. He just kept staring. Then he pushed the man in the cowboy boots and the two men darted out the door.

It took Justin a moment to move. There was a strange stillness outside. He walked toward the door and opened it wide. There were the two criminals standing with their backs to him, frozen in place. Just like Lucky.

Jackie and Nick were facing them. And so was Zack. And so were Margaret and Meredith. And there was Ryan with his skateboard and a bunch of kids, younger and older, Justin didn't recognize. They were all gathered in a semicircle surrounding the two outlaws.

Three policemen were also there, talking like crazy on walkie-talkies. A police helicopter zoomed low overhead. The officers walked up to the two men and handcuffed them. There was no resistance.

As the police made sure Justin was unharmed and escorted the men away, all the Adirondack kids

75

gathered around Justin and the two cats. Margaret cradled Dax and Zack held tiny Hudson.

Justin embraced Jackie and Nick. "How did you know where I was?" he asked.

Jackie smiled. "It was easy. We followed your trail."

Justin looked puzzled. "What trail?"

"Popcorn!" said Nick. He held up his bag. "It was flying out of your bag while you were running."

"Nick was the one who saw you racing down the platform and figured something was wrong," explained Zack. "So we all pitched in to see what was up. We didn't know we were putting together a posse to catch some bandits."

"Just like they did in North Creek a hundred years ago," said Jackie.

"I was only looking for Dax," said Justin. He reached out to pet her as she still rested contentedly in Margaret's arms. "I didn't expect all this to happen."

The train whistle blew and began its journey up the track with President Roosevelt and more than 300 happy passengers aboard.

"I'm sorry, you guys," said Justin. "You all missed riding the train with the President."

"Wassup up, Dawg?" It was Ryan. He slapped Justin on the back. "You're in North Creek now," he said, "where we all take care of each other."

76

CHAPTER XV

Just in Time

Justin, Jackie and Nick were packed, and along with Dax were all ready to go. They stood out on the lawn of the Casey homestead with Zack and his mom, waiting for Justin's parents to arrive from Eagle Bay.

"Thanks for having us this weekend," Justin said.

"Yes, thank you very much," said Jackie. There was an awkward pause and she elbowed Nick.

"Oh, yes, thank you," Nick said. "Everything was great – especially all the skulls in the museum."

"You are all very welcome," said Mrs. Casey. "We hope you will come back and visit us again soon. I know Zachary loved it."

Zack grinned.

A brown station wagon pulled into the driveway. It was Mr. Casey. He had been at the depot finishing up business with the law officials.

He emerged from the wagon still dressed in his conductor's uniform. "What a day," he said, as he greeted them. He looked at Justin. "I'm glad I could get back to say good-bye before you all left for home."

"What did they do with the bandits?" asked Zack. "Where did they come from? Did they find any money?"

"Whoa, slow down," said Mr. Casey. "We don't know a lot yet, but there is some information."

"I'm very interested in all this as well," confessed Mrs. Casey.

Mr. Casey sat on the front porch steps to explain. "It seems the two of them were involved in the robbery together all right," he began. "The one drifter picked up a part-time summer job helping out the crew painting the buildings at the station."

"Now I remember that guy," said Zack. "He was the one watching us funny at the depot right after we first found the cowboy boot."

Mr. Casey nodded. "Well, he got to know some of the railroad staff and learned the robbery routine and fed his hidden buddy the information. Neither of them seemed very smart. They're not from the area, and with the quick response of law enforcement, they had nowhere to run. One of them nearly drowned in the river. There were holes in his raft and he apparently doesn't know how to swim."

Justin and Nick looked at Dax.

"He also had a serious bruise on his chest, an infected cut on one of his legs and has a terrible case of poison ivy," said Mr. Casey. "He was in pretty rough shape and needed medical treatment immediately. They are both in jail now."

"So that's how they knew where to look for the

78

boot?" said Zack. "The one guy knew who I was and where we lived. That's kind of creepy."

"They wanted to get back the evidence," said Jackie.

"Maybe his foot was sore," suggested Nick. "The Adirondacks are a tough place to run around in your bare feet."

They all laughed.

Jackie looked at Justin. "It must have been awful being trapped in the section shed with the two of them," she said.

Justin nodded. "It's the buddy system for me from now on," he said. "Going anywhere!"

"Well, you were fortunate, Justin, but it turns out they were quite harmless," said Mr. Casey. "That's why they couldn't bring themselves to hurt even Hudson. They simply thought they would pull a fast one in a small town and make a few easy bucks – and they were very wrong."

"Did they find any of the money?" asked Nick. "Or is there treasure buried somewhere in the woods?"

"The police haven't recovered any of the money yet," said Mr. Casey. "So it could be buried somewhere out there, or maybe the thieves spent it."

Justin sighed. "Well, the most important thing is Dax found Hudson and now she can be adopted and have a whole railroad family."

The train whistle blew off in the distance.

"Is it that time already?" said Mr. Casey.

He reached into his pocket for his watch. He popped it open, looked at it, and snapped it shut.

"Yes," he said. "It's another special party run, and it's right on schedule."

Justin looked curiously at the timepiece. "I thought your watch was silver," he said.

"My watch *is* silver," said Mr. Casey. "This isn't my watch." He handed it to Justin. "This is *your* watch."

Justin was so happy, he didn't know what to say. He really thought he would never see the watch again. He didn't even hear Mr. Casey explain when the thieves emptied their pockets at the depot, there was not any cash, but the outstanding gold antique timepiece on its gold chain clattered across the table.

A jeep pulled into the driveway.

Justin popped open the watch to see the welcome face looking back up at him. The big hand was on the XII and the little hand was on the VI. "Right on time," he said, and smiled. And he snapped the watch shut.

Epilogue

Justin was laying on his stomach in bed and staring out the open window of the sleeping porch back at camp in Eagle Bay. He was simply listening to the familiar summer sounds of boats and seaplanes and happy voices out on Fourth Lake. Dax was curled up asleep next to him, on the back of the wicker chair.

What a weekend, he thought.

He wondered what made camp so special.

Was it because he didn't live here all year-round? That couldn't be it. Jackie lived here all year, and she loved it. And so did his cousin and all his new friends at North Creek.

He sighed.

It really doesn't matter, he thought. *This is just one of the best places on the whole earth.*

But he decided he'd had enough adventure to last him for a while. And he was tired. Just plain tired. Maybe he would even take a nap. He adjusted his pillow and laid down his head.

The phone rang.

"Justin, it's for you," called his mom. "I think it's Nick."

He even beat Dax down the stairs.

Justin was staring out the window
of the sleeping porch.

DAX FACTS

Theodore Roosevelt was born in New York City on October 27, 1858.

While frail with asthma as a child, Roosevelt grew up to be quite strong and athletic and in college participated in sports like rowing, boxing and ice-skating.

Theodore Roosevelt at 11 years old. As a boy, he loved to read adventure stories. *Photo appears by permission and courtesy of Theodore Roosevelt Collection, Harvard College Library*

As a young boy, he loved to read adventure tales and seemed to enjoy stories set in the great outdoors, especially those written by Mayne Reid. He also kept a journal and drew sketches of birds and mammals.

While growing up in New York City, he obtained the skull of a seal and with two cousins began what they called the Roosevelt Museum of Natural History. For a while, the Museum was set up in his bedroom where he even kept small dead animals in his bureau drawers! When he was 13, he was allowed to take taxidermy lessons. He credits the experience for his ongoing interest in collecting specimens for preservation.

This love for nature was evident throughout Roosevelt's entire life. In fact, when he became President of the United States, he even let his own children bring pets into the White House, including a pony and some snakes.

Roosevelt had only been the Vice President of the United States for six months when President William McKinley was shot at the World's Fair in Buffalo, New York. When it was learned that McKinley might not live, Roosevelt was on vacation and hiking on Mt. Marcy in the Adirondack Mountains. He traveled all night and at 5 a.m. arrived at the North Creek Depot where he learned by telegram McKinley had died early that morning.

Theodore Roosevelt once said, "There is a delight in the hardy life of the open." *Photo appears by permission and courtesy Theodore Roosevelt Collection, Harvard College Library*

On September 14, 1901, Theodore Roosevelt became the 26th President of the United States. At only 42 years of age, he was also the youngest man to ever become President.

Mike Cronin and his team of horses carried Theodore Roosevelt the final miles of his wild nighttime journey from Mt. Marcy to the North Creek station where he received a telegram and learned President McKinley had died early in the morning. The carriage is on display at the Adirondack Museum in Blue Mountain Lake, New York. *Photo appears by permission and courtesy of the Adirondack Museum, Blue Mountain Lake, New York. To learn more about the Adirondack Museum, contact www.adirondackmuseum.org.*

President Theodore Roosevelt in the White House in 1903. *Photo appears by permission and courtesy of Theodore Roosevelt Collection, Harvard College Library*

Vintage photograph of the North Creek Railway Depot taken March 4, 1934 by John Cornwall. *Photo appears courtesy of Helen Cornwall.*

The **North Creek Railroad Station** complex is located at the northern end of the hamlet of North Creek and on the west bank of the Hudson River in the Town of Johnsburg in the Adirondacks.

The station appears today almost exactly as it did when it was first constructed in 1871. Its existence helped make possible the recreational and industrial development of the Central Adirondacks.

The North Creek Railroad Station is perhaps best known as the place where Theodore Roosevelt learned via telegram that President McKinley had died, making Roosevelt the 26th President of the United States.

For more information on the history of North Creek Railroad Station and the Upper Hudson River Railroad, contact Upper Hudson River Railroad, 3 Railroad Place, P.O. Box 424, North Creek, New York 22853, or visit www.UHRR.com. Also see the PBS television production: Great Scenic Railroad Journeys – 175 Years of American Railroads. Visit www.pbs.org.

 # DAX FACTS

Locomotive No. 5019 was built in 1962 by Alco in Schenectady, New York for the Delaware and Hudson Railroad. Used mostly for hauling freight trains, the road switching locomotive weighs nearly a quarter of a million pounds, or 120 tons.

The **Hudson River** that flows alongside the tracks of the Upper Hudson River Railroad at North Creek is actually 315 miles long. The river begins in the Adirondack Mountains at Lake Tear of the Clouds on New York state's highest peak, Mount Marcy.

The river runs all the way past the capital of New York state, Albany, and finally pours into the Atlantic Ocean at New York City. The Hudson River is named after the English explorer, Henry Hudson, who in 1609 was the first European to sail up the major waterway.

The Upper Hudson River Railroad runs seasonal round-trips from the North Creek Depot to the Riverside Station on 8.5 miles of track running alongside the Hudson River in the Adirondack Mountains. *Photo by Gary VanRiper*

DAX FACTS

The **Roman Numeral** system was invented by the ancient Romans as a way of writing numbers. The seven basic symbols used to make the numbers include **I** for 1, **V** for 5, **X** for 10, **L** for 50, **C** for 100, **D** for 500 and **M** for 1,000. In the Roman Numeral system, all other numbers are made from adding or subtracting some combination of these seven basic symbols.

Roman Numerals are not used much today and are most often seen on the faces of watches and clocks or for listing topics in a written outline. Does your town clock have Roman Numerals?

In the *Adirondack Kids #4 – The Great Train Robbery*, Roman Numerals were used to number each chapter!

What follows are Roman Numerals from 1 to 1,000.

1 = **I**	11 = **XI**	30 = **XXX**
2 = **II**	12 = **XII**	40 = **XL**
3 = **III**	13 = **XIII**	50 = **L**
4 = **IV**	14 = **XIV**	60 = **LX**
5 = **V**	15 = **XV**	70 = **LXX**
6 = **VI**	16 = **XVI**	80 = **LXXX**
7 = **VII**	17 = **XVII**	90 = **XC**
8 = **VIII**	18 = **XVIII**	100 = **C**
9 = **IX**	19 = **XIX**	500 = **D**
10 = **X**	20 = **XX**	1,000 = **M**

About the Authors

Gary and Justin VanRiper are a father and son writing team residing in Camden, New York of the Tug Hill region with their family and cats, Socks and Dax. They spend many summer and autumn days at camp on Fourth Lake in the Adirondacks.

The Adirondack Kids® began as a short writing exercise when Justin was in third grade. Encouraged after a public reading of an early draft at a Parents As Reading Partners (PARP) program in the Camden Central School District, the project grew into a middle reader chapter book series. *The Adirondack Kids*® #4 is their fourth book.

About the Illustrators

Carol McCurn VanRiper is a professional photographer and illustrator who lives and works in Camden, New York. She is also the wife and mother of co-authors, Gary and Justin VanRiper, and inherited the job as publicist when *The Adirondack Kids*® progressed from a family dream to a small company. *The Adirondack Kids*® #4 is her first book.

Susan Loeffler is a freelance illustrator who lives and works in Upstate New York.

The Adirondack Kids® #1

Justin Robert is ten years old and likes computers, biking and peanut butter cups. But his passion is animals. When an uncommon pair of Common Loons takes up residence on Fourth Lake near the family camp, he will do anything he can to protect them.

The Adirondack Kids® #2
Rescue on Bald Mountain

Justin Robert and Jackie Salsberry are on a special mission. It is Fourth of July weekend in the Adirondacks and time for the annual ping-pong ball drop at Inlet. Their best friend, Nick Barnes, has won the opportunity to release the balls from a seaplane, but there is just one problem. He is afraid of heights. With a single day remaining before the big event, Justin and Jackie decide there is only one way to help Nick overcome his fear. Climb Bald Mountain!

The Adirondack Kids® #3
The Lost Lighthouse

Justin Robert, Jackie Salsberry and Nick Barnes are fishing under sunny Adirondack skies when a sudden and violent storm chases them off Fourth Lake and into an unfamiliar forest – a forest that has harbored a secret for more than 100 years.

The Adirondack Kids® #5
Islands in the Sky

Justin Robert, Jackie Salsberry and Nick Barnes head for the Adirondack high peaks wilderness – while Justin's calico cat, Dax, embarks on an unexpected tour of the Adirondack Park.

The Adirondack Kids®
Story & Coloring Book
Runaway Dax

Artist Susan Loeffler brings a favorite Adirondack Kids® character – Dax – to life in 32 coloring book illustrations set to a story-line for young readers written by Adirondack Kids® co-creator and author, Justin VanRiper.

Over **60,000** Adirondack Kids Books in Print!

On sale wherever great books on the Adirondacks are found or on **The Adirondack Kids®** official web site
www.ADIRONDACKKIDS.com